Wide Eye™

Spotty Little Hoot

99

Natterjack Toad

Rangatang

Flea

The Fireflies

Wide Eye

BBC CHILDREN'S BOOKS
Published by the Penguin Group
Penguin Books Ltd, 80 Strand, London
WC2R 0RL, England
Penguin Books Australia Ltd, 250 Camberwell Road,
Camberwell, Victoria 3124, Australia
Published by BBC Children's Books, 2005

10 9 8 7 6 5 4 3 2 1
Written by Jackie Andrews
Based on the television series

ISBN 1 4059 0042 3
Printed in Italy

"Wake up, Little Hoot!"
said Flea one morning.
"Let's play!"

"I'b dot well, Flea,"
whispered Little Hoot.
"By throad hurds.
Aaaahtchooo!"

“What you need is a bowl of blackberry broth,” said Flea. “I’ll just go and get what I need.”

She picked up a basket
and skipped away.
"Oh, doh," groaned
Little Hoot.

“This’ll make you feel much better, Little Hoot!” said Flea, as she mixed and stirred the broth.

“It looks yucky to me,” said Little Hoot.

Just then, Wide
Eye swooped in.
"Hello, Wide Eye!
Little Hoot's
poorly, and I'm
looking after him!"
said Flea.
"Twit-a-woo!" said
Wide Eye. "You've
got a temperature,
Little Hoot."

“My special broth will soon cool him down,” said Flea.

"What have you put in it, Flea?" asked Wide Eye. "Er… this and that," said Flea.

"It's not a good idea to eat or drink something you're not sure of," said Wide Eye. "It might make Little Hoot feel worse, not better."

"Hoo, hoo!" said Little Hoot.
"I feel very itchy."
"Look! SPOTS!" squeaked Flea.
"Don't scratch them, Little Hoot," said Wide Eye. "I'll go get something to help. And don't touch any of that broth!"

Mother Natterjack popped into the treehouse a little later. "Wide Eye has sent me to look after you, Little Hoot," she said. "I've brought some dock leaves for your spots, and some lovely... worm stew!"

"Ughhh!"
Little Hoot dived under the bedclothes. Flea suddenly remembered something important she had to do.

"Wha-haay!"
"Whee!"
"Ooooh!"

Suddenly, the treehouse was full of little toads, jumping and bouncing over Little Hoot's bed.

"Oh, no!" groaned Little Hoot.
"I feel sick."
"Hop it!" said Mother Natterjack to her noisy children. "Leave Little Hoot in peace!"
'Owww! We wanted to play nurses!"

Mother Natterjack fed Little Hoot the worm stew and rubbed soothing dock leaves on his spots.

Soon Little Hoot was feeling more comfortable.

"Thank you, Mother Natterjack," he said, sleepily, as she left.

When Wide Eye returned, he brought Little Hoot some cool, fresh water from the Natterjack spring.

"Go to sleep now, Little Hoot," said Wide Eye. "I'll be here."

"You won't sing to me, will you?" murmured Little Hoot.

"Certainly not!"

That night, while Little Hoot slept, Batwing came and hovered over his bed, flapping her little wings to cool his itchy spots.

In the morning, Little Hoot felt as good as new.

"Come on, Flea," he said, bouncing out of bed. "I feel fine. Let's play!"

But Flea didn't move.

"Dohh. I'b dot well. And I'b all hot and itchy," she moaned.

"Poor Flea!" said Little Hoot. "Don't worry, I'll look after you. I'll get Mother Natterjack to make you some nice worm stew. And I'll sing you a lullaby..."

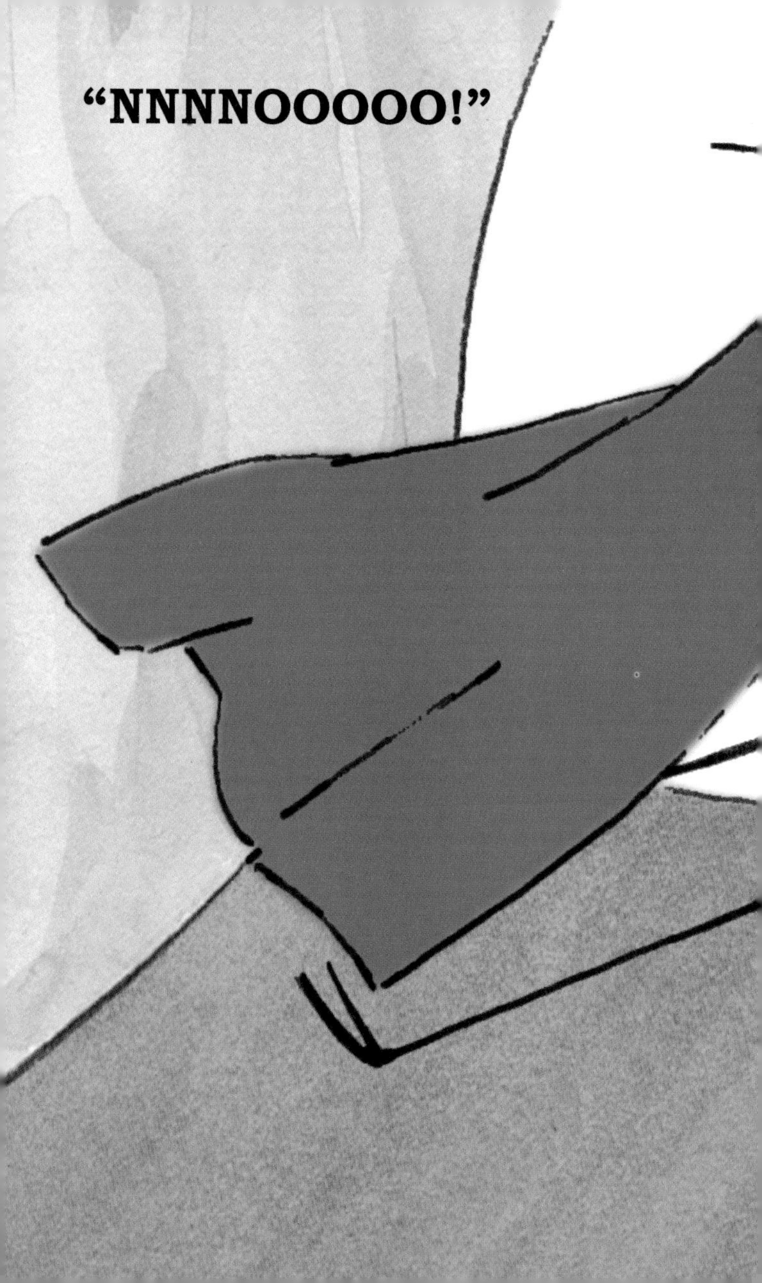
"NNNNOOOOO!"

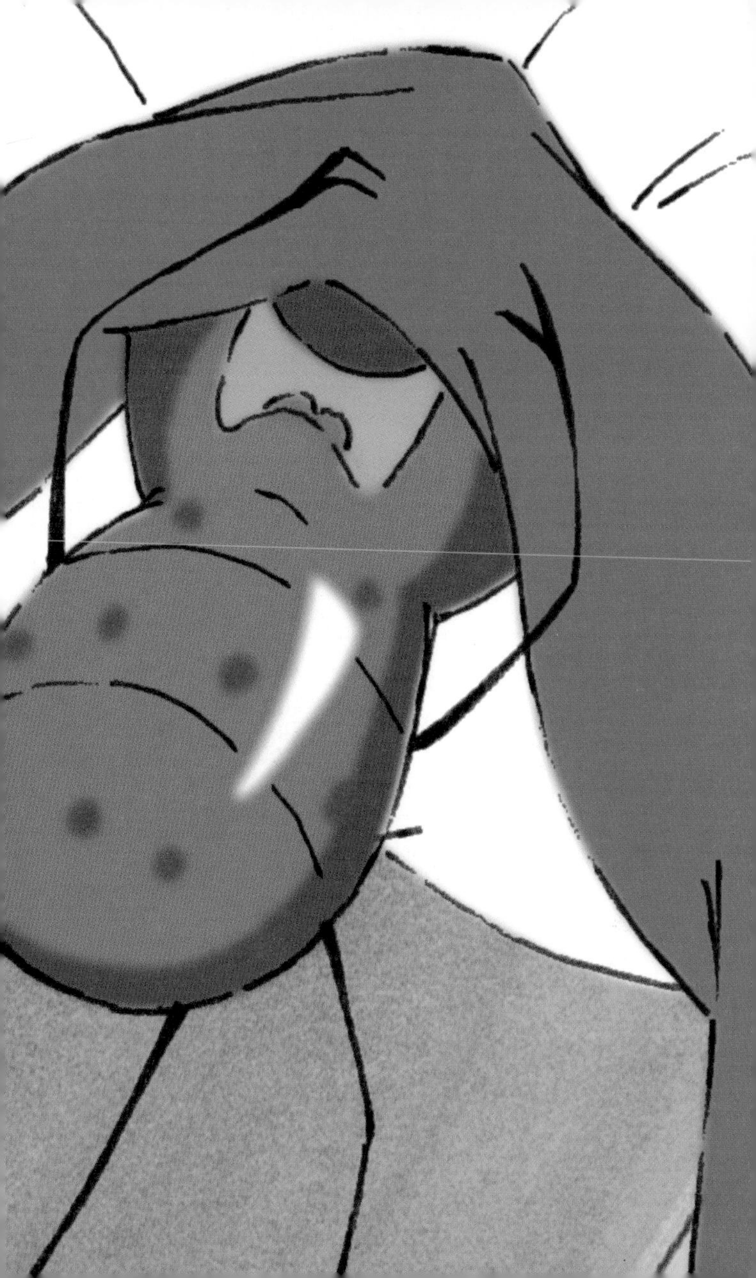

Little Hoot

Flea

Hetty

Batwing

Baby Komodo

Conchita